L(')
1980

Reinach
Shoes

Juv.

DATE DUE		
JAN. 2 4 1981	NOV. 8 1984	
FEB. 1 2 1981	NOV. 2 9 1984	
FEB. 2 8 1981	JAN. 1 2 1984	
APR. 1 8 1981	SEP. 2 8 1985	
	NOV. 1 5 1986	
APR. 3 0 1981		
JUL. 2 5 1981	JUN. 0 4 1988	
SEP. 2 6	JUL. 3 1 1989	
DEC. - 5 1981	JUN. 2 2 1991	
MAY 7 1988	AUG. 1 7 1991	
JUL. 1 6 1983	NOV. 2 8 1992	
	APR 0 4 2002	

THIS SWEET PICKLES® BOOK BELONGS TO

In the world of *Sweet Pickles,* each animal gets into a pickle because of an all too human personality trait.

This book is about Accusing Alligator who blames everything and everybody for anything that happens.

Other Books in the Sweet Pickles Series

Library of Congress Cataloging in Publication Data

Reinach, Jacquelyn.
  Who stole Alligator's shoe.

  (Sweet Pickles series)
  SUMMARY: Alligator blames everybody but herself
when she can't find her left shoe.
  [1. Alligators—Fiction] I. Hefter, Richard.
II. Title. III. Series.
PZ7.R2747Wh   [E]   77-7251
ISBN 0-03-021431-9

Printed in the United States of America

Weekly Reader Books' Edition

Weekly Reader Books presents

WHO STOLE ALLIGATOR'S SHOE?

Written by Jacquelyn Reinach
Illustrated by Richard Hefter
Edited by Ruth Lerner Perle

Holt, Rinehart and Winston · New York

One rainy morning, Alligator slept right through the alarm clock and didn't wake up until eight-thirty.

Alligator was supposed to be up at seven. She was supposed to turn up the heat and collect the garbage and tidy the lobby at the Tower Apartments.

"Dumb clock!" she yelled. "You didn't wake me up and it's all your fault I'm late for work!"

Alligator ran to shut the window. It was stuck and wouldn't close. "You dumb window!" she shouted. "What's the matter with you?"

Alligator grabbed a hammer and started to bang the window shut. She missed the wood and hit her foot instead. "OUCH!" she shrieked in pain. "YOU MISERABLE HAMMER!"

She threw the hammer down. It went crashing through the window glass. SPLAT!

"*Now* look what you made me do!" cried Alligator. "I'm getting all wet! I'd better get dressed."

When she went to get dressed, Alligator couldn't find her left shoe.

She opened her door and shouted into the hallway, "Okay, everybody, who stole my left shoe?"

Stork called from the top floor. "I can tell you about your left shoe in three words!"

"Well?" screamed Alligator.

"I don't know," answered Stork.

"Tough luck!" shrieked Nightingale from the fourth floor. "Who would want your smelly old shoe?"

"This is outrageous!" muttered Alligator. "Someone has definitely stolen my left shoe!"

"I doubt it," said Dog from the second floor.
"Me too!" called Iguana from the third floor.

From the first floor apartment, Yak said, "I was saying to Rabbit just last night, that it's hard to keep track of shoes sometimes. And he said to me, 'That's very silly. Shoes are either on your feet or in the closet.' And I said to him, 'I suppose that's true. *But,* if a shoe is *not* on your foot and...' "

"Oh, stop yakking," snapped Alligator. "You never get to the point. You never have a point to get to."

Alligator went out to the lobby to look for the thief who took her left shoe.

She saw the mop and pail in the middle of the lobby floor and was furious. "I would have put that stuff away last night," she scowled, "if they didn't keep me so busy around here. It's all their fault!"

Alligator hurried to clean up the lobby. Her tail hit the mop, the mop hit the pail, sudsy water sloshed out, and Alligator went sliding across the lobby floor. "Help! Help!" she cried. "Who spilled the water?" She slid out the door, down the steps and into the front driveway. Just then Fish came zooming up to deliver the newspapers.

"Look out!" shouted Alligator. "You almost ran over my tail!"

"Hey, don't blow a gasket," called Fish. She flipped the newspapers to Alligator and swerved away.

"Wise guy!" yelled Alligator.

Alligator brushed herself off and sat down to count all the bad things that had just happened. "Seven bad things," she grumped, "including my left shoe. Everybody knows bad things come in sevens!"

She opened a newspaper. "I'd better see what my stars say," she thought. "Maybe this is not my day."

Alligator read her horoscope.

THIS IS NOT YOUR DAY.

"I knew it!" she cried. "Now I *know* why nothing is going right!" She continued reading. TAKE A WALK. YOU'LL FIND THINGS BETTER.

"Ah, ha!" said Alligator. "That means if I take a walk, I'll find my left shoe!"

So Alligator went for a walk in the park.

The rain had stopped.

Bear was sitting under a tree quietly playing his banjo.

Elephant was buttering slices of bread.

Pig was hitting a ball to Dog.

Alligator hobbled up to Bear. "Where's my left shoe?" she demanded.

"Excuse me, but I don't know," whispered Bear.

"Well, what *do* you know?" snapped Alligator. "It's certainly not music!"

"I'm sorry I can't help you," sighed Bear. "Maybe your shoe is somewhere else in the park. Excuse me."

Alligator marched along the path looking for her left shoe.

Pig called out, "Hey, hey, hey, Alligator. The sun came out. It's a beautiful day. Here, catch!"

Pig tossed the ball. It bopped Alligator on the tail.

"You did that on purpose!" said Alligator. "Anyway, I wasn't ready. I'm looking for my left shoe."

"I'm sure you'll find it," smiled Pig. "But let's have fun now."

Pig picked up the ball and threw it to Dog. Dog spun around and shot it to Alligator. Alligator ducked. The ball went by.

"That's weird," called Dog. "Why didn't you catch the ball this time?"

"It's your fault," said Alligator. "You're throwing wild. I can't catch a wild throw."

"It looked fine to me," said Pig.

"Never mind," said Alligator. "I don't want to play ball. You guys are always messing up!"

She kept going, looking for her left shoe.

Elephant smiled, "Hi, Alligator. Want a sandwich?"

"No!" grumbled Alligator. "I want my left shoe!"

"We're taking pictures of our sandwiches," giggled Zebra. "Mine is a banana sandwich!"

Everyone applauded.

Alligator ignored them. "Someone has stolen my left shoe," she announced, "and I want it. *Now!*"

"See you later, Alligator!" called Kangaroo.

"Hmmmph!" grunted Alligator. She walked away and sat down to rest.

Just then, Yak drove by.

"…As I was saying," called Yak, "if a shoe is *not* on your foot and it's *not* in the closet, and it's somebody else's left shoe, and you happen to trip over it in the lobby where somebody forgot to put it away, *and* she forgot to put away the mop and the pail also, and you fell on them and hurt your nose, what then, I ask?"

"You mean my left shoe has been in the lobby all this time?" screeched Alligator.

"That's the point I was getting to," called Yak, as he drove away.

"Why didn't you tell me sooner?" cried Alligator.
"I've had such a terrible day!
"AND IT'S ALL YOUR FAULT!"

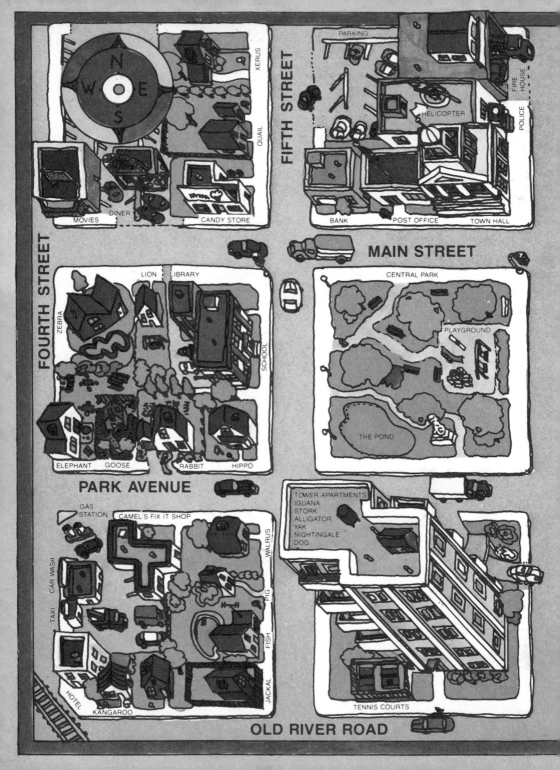